One Day in the Eucalyptus, Eucalyptus Tree

Story by Daniel Bernstrom Pictures by Brendan Wenzel

KT KATHERINE TEGEN BOOKS
An Imprint of HarperCollins Publishers

One day in the leaves
of the eucalyptus tree
hung a scare in the air
where no eye could see,

EUCALYPTUS

when along **skipped** a boy
with a whirly-twirly toy,
to the shade of the eucalyptus,
eucalyptus tree.

Down, down

slid the snake

from the leaves of the tree

and **gobbled** up the boy
with his whirly-twirly toy,

one day in the **eucalyptus**,
eucalyptus tree.

"I'll bet," said the boy,
in the belly dark and deep,
"that you're still very hungry
and there's more you can eat."

"Do you think," said the snake
to the boy with the toy,
"that there's room for something **yummy**
with you inside my tummy?"

Cheep, cheep came a chirp
from the leaves of the tree.

Oh! A bird with a worm in
a game of hide-and-seek.

Sneaky-slidey **zipped** the snake
from his place in the leaves

and **gobbled** up the bird
and her ooey-gooey worm,

one day in the **eucalyptus,**
eucalyptus tree.

"I'll bet," said the boy,
in the belly dark and deep,
"that you're still very hungry,
and there's more you can eat."

Purr, purr came a stir from
the leaves of the tree.

Oh! A cat in a nap on his
furry, furry back.

Under-over slid the snake
from his place in the leaves
and **gobbled** up the cat
in his dozy-cozy nap,

one day in the **eucalyptus**,
eucalyptus tree.

"Oh surely, very surely,
Mr. Snake," said the boy,
"there is room. Still more room.
So much more to enjoy!"

Crinkle, wrinkle came a
rustle from the leaves of the tree.

Oh! A sloth cloaked in moss,
sipping leafy, leafy tea.

Wiggle-waggle
stretched the snake
from his place in the leaves
and **gobbled** up the sloth
clothed in fuzzy-wuzzy moss,

one day in the **eucalyptus,
eucalyptus** tree.

"I'll bet," said the boy,
in the belly dark and deep,
"that you're still very hungry,
that there's more you can eat."

Slurp, buuuuurrrrp! came a belch from the leaves of the tree.

Oh! An ape eating grapes, lounging like a queen.

Twist-twist bent the snake from his place in the leaves

and **gobbled** up the ape and her munchy bunch of grapes,

one day in the **eucalyptus, eucalyptus** tree.

"Oh surely, very surely,
Mr. Snake," said the boy,
"there is room. Still more room.
So much more to enjoy!"

Munch, munch came a crunch from the leaves of the tree. Oh! A rare kind of bear munching tasty, tasty greens.

Up, up snaked the snake from his place in the leaves and **gobbled** up the bear with the qually-wally hair,

one day in the **eucalyptus, eucalyptus** tree.

"Do you think," asked the snake
to the boy with the toy,
"I should take one more **bite**
while my tummy feels so tight?"

"Oh surely, very surely,
Mr. Snake," said the boy.
"There is room, so much room.
Go ahead, please enjoy!"

Buzz, buzz hummed a noise
from the leaves of the tree.
Oh! A hive full of bees,
    dancing happily.

Creeky-eeky inched the snake
from his place in the leaves
and **gobbled** up the hive
and the bumbling bees inside,

one day in the **eucalyptus**,
eucalyptus tree.

"I'll bet," said the boy,
in the belly dark and deep,
"that you're still very hungry,
that there's more you can eat."

"No," said the snake.

"Oh surely, very surely, Mr. Snake," said the boy, "there is room. Still more room . . ."

"No," said the snake.

"Something small?" asked the boy.

Sniff, sniff hissed the snake
from his place in the leaves.

Oh! A fruit, a small fruit,
swaying in the breeze.
And on that piece of fruit,
that plummy-chummy fruit,

Gurgle-gurgle came a blurble
from that belly deep and full.

STRETCH!

STRETCH!

STRETCH!

Out **whizzed** the fly,
Out **rolled** the fruit,
Out **buzzed** the hive,
Out **ran** the bear,
Out **swung** the ape,
Out **slunk** the sloth,
Out **dashed** the cat,
Out **flew** the bird,
Out **slimed** the worm.

And out **skipped** the boy
with his whirly-twirly toy.

And . . .

"Ohhh," **moaned** the snake,
"I've a crummy tummyache."

One day in the **eucalyptus,**
eucalyptus tree.

To Laken and Hudson
—D.B.

For the Kopila kids
—B.W.

Katherine Tegen Books is an imprint of HarperCollins Publishers.　　One Day in the Eucalyptus, Eucalyptus Tree　　Text copyright © 2016 by Daniel Bernstrom　　Illustrations copyright © 2016 by Brendan Wenzel
All rights reserved. Manufactured in China.　　No part of this book may be used or reproduced in any manner whatsoever without written permission except in the case of brief quotations embodied in critical articles
and reviews. For information address HarperCollins Children's Books, a division of HarperCollins Publishers, 195 Broadway, New York, NY 10007　　www.harpercollinschildrens.com　　ISBN 978-0-06-235485-3
The artist used everything imaginable to create the digital illustrations for this book.　　Typography by Rachel Zegar　　16　17　18　19　20　SCP　10　9　8　7　6　5　4　3　2　1　❖　First Edition